Nat the Cat

the

Cat

Takes a Nap

By Jarrett Lerner

Ready-to-Read

Simon Spotlight

New York   London   Toronto   Sydney   New Delhi

For Florence and Sir Tobin

SIMON SPOTLIGHT
An imprint of Simon & Schuster Children's Publishing Division
1230 Avenue of the Americas, New York, New York 10020
This Simon Spotlight edition January 2023
Copyright © 2023 by Jarrett Lerner
For information about special discounts for bulk purchases, please
contact Simon & Schuster Special Sales at 1-866-506-1949 or
business@simonandschuster.com.
Manufactured in United States of America 0323 LAK
2 4 6 8 10 9 7 5 3
This book has been cataloged by the Library of Congress.
ISBN 978-1-6659-1891-6 (hc)
ISBN 978-1-6659-1890-9 (pbk)
ISBN 978-1-6659-1892-3 (ebook)

This is Nat.

Nat is a cat.

Nat the Cat
is taking
a nap.

Now,
Nat the Cat
is TRYING
to take a nap.

Nat the Cat
is trying
to take a nap.

Nat the Cat
is REALLY trying
to take a nap.

Nat the Cat
is REALLY taking
a nap!

Hooray for Nat!

Nat the Cat
has called for
his brother.

This is Pat the Rat.
Pat the Rat
is the brother of
Nat the Cat.

Pat the Rat is NOT my brother.

Nat the Cat is mad
at Pat the Rat.

Nat the Cat
is NOT mad.

Is Nat the Cat sad?

I just want to take a nap! Please, just let me take a nap!

Please be quiet,
Nat the Cat!
Pat the Rat
is taking a nap.

ZZZZZZ...

ZZZZZZ...